NANNYCATCH
CHRONICLES

Published simultaneously in 2005 in Great Britain and Canada by
TRADEWIND BOOKS LIMITED www.tradewindbooks.com
Distribution and representation in the UK by TURNAROUND www.turnaround-uk.com

This book has been printed on 100% ancient-forest-free paper (100% post-consumer
recycled, processed chlorine and acid free) using vegetable-based inks.

Book design by Elisa Gutiérrez

Library and Archives Canada Cataloguing in Publication
Heneghan, James, 1930-
    The Nannycatch chronicles / by James Heneghan & Bruce
McBay ; illustrated by Geraldo Valerio.

ISBN 1-896580-56-4

    I. McBay, Bruce, 1946- II. Valerio, Geraldo III. Title.
PS8565.E581N36 2005   jC813'.54   C2005-902341-4

Printed and bound in Canada   10   9   8   7   6   5   4   3   2   I

The publisher thanks the Canada Council for the Arts
and the British Columbia Arts Council for their support.

James Heneghan and Bruce McBay

NANNYCATCH
CHRONICLES

illustrated by Geraldo Valério

PUBLISHER'S WARNING

Everything dies: flowers, trees, elephants,
bees, hamsters, turtles, dolphins, dogs, cats...
Everything.
Nothing lives forever.
Everyone knows this.
Young readers, however, should guard against this
book falling into the hands of grown-ups, many of
whom get quite upset whenever the subject of death
is mentioned.
Don't ask us why.

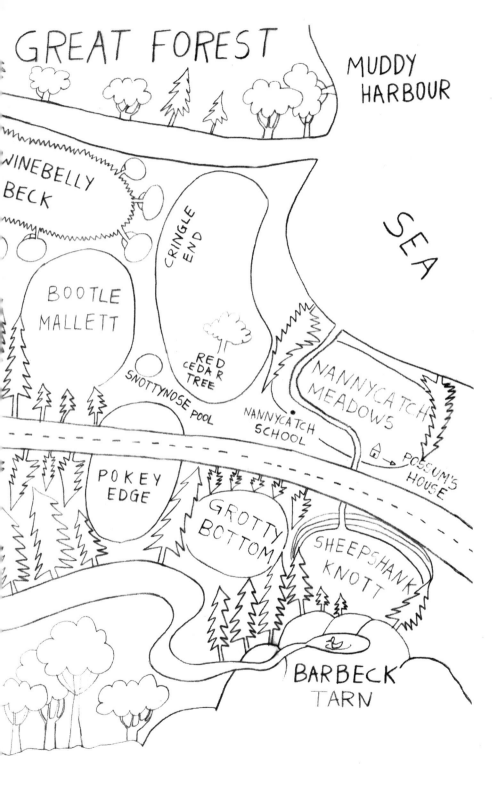

CONTENTS

CHAPTER 1

POSSUM'S DREADFUL BIRTHDAY PARTY

It was Possum's birthday, and he was having a party. When it was time for his friends to arrive, he stood outside waiting to greet them, but the forest and fields were empty; not a creature stirred. "I hope they didn't forget my birthday party," he said to his friends Chipmunk and Robin, who were perched on a branch over his head.

Possum lived in The Great Forest, in an old oak tree, in a pretty little spot called Nannycatch Meadows.

"I don't see anyone coming," said Robin. "Did you remember to send invitations to everyone?"

"Of course," said Possum.

Robin flicked her tail. "Then I am sure they will be here any minute."

"I will climb up beside you and watch for them," said Possum. He grabbed his binoculars and climbed into the thick, leafy canopy where his hammock swung between two stout branches. Soon Possum could see Raccoon loping through last year's brown leaves towards his place. He spotted his friend Badger poking his head

out of a rusty pipe that had been left behind after the New Highway was finished. And there was Dormouse darting through the grass, looking over his shoulder to make sure Brown Owl wasn't about to swoop down and gobble him up.

"They're coming," said Possum with a sigh of relief.

Through his binoculars, Possum could see the New Highway in the distance, a broad ribbon of glaring concrete cutting a path through The Great Forest, through the neighbourhoods of Boggle Hole, Pokey Edge and Biskey Fen. The New Highway had changed everyone's lives in the three communities. "Don't go near the New Highway!" mothers warned their children. But the children needed no warning: the roaring monsters with night-blinding eyes were scary enough to keep them away.

Now, on this bright spring afternoon, Possum could see his Uncle Possum strutting along beside the Highway, making his way to his nephew's birthday party. Uncle Possum lived in Grotty Bottom, not far from Nannycatch Meadows. Wheeled monsters swept by him with a roar. Uncle Possum shook his walking-stick angrily at the Highway monsters and lashed out viciously at anything obstructing his path, be it badger, bird or bush.

Just slightly ahead of Uncle Possum, Weasel shuffled slowly along, taking his time. He was nervous about the Highway traffic. Uncle Possum soon caught up with him and slashed the air with his walking-stick. "Out of my way, Weasel!"

Weasel jumped fearfully, slipped off the curb, fell onto the Highway and—whoops! A big truck ran over Weasel.

Possum dropped his binoculars and covered his eyes with his paws. He couldn't look. Weasel was flatter than a flatworm.

Possum turned to Robin. "Weasel just got flattened on the New Highway!"

"That's dreadful!" cried Robin.

"MOST UPSETTING," said Pigeon, who had a tendency to talk in headlines. He had just flown down from a high branch. "SAW THE WHOLE THING. MOST UPSETTING. WEASEL CARELESS." Pigeon worked for the Pigeon Post and also delivered the daily newspaper.

Possum said, "This is terrible. Poor Weasel! What am I to do about my birthday party?"

"Search me," said Chipmunk.

"There's nothing much any of us can do," said Robin, wiping away a tear. "We should just continue with our plans. Weasel would wish us all to carry on, I'm sure."

"It will be a dreadful birthday party," said Possum, as his friends crowded into his hollow-tree home.

"Listen, everyone," said Possum, after all this guests had arrived, "Robin has sad news."

Robin perched on the handle of the kettle where everyone could see her. "Sad news, indeed. Weasel will not be here with us today. He met his end on the New Highway. He is no longer with us." Her eyes ran with tears. "Weasel, alas, is no more."

Everyone groaned. Many wept.

"MOST UPSETTING," said Pigeon.

"How sad," said Chipmunk.

"I saw the whole thing," said Hawk. "It was shocking."

4

"A tragedy, indeed," said Uncle Possum, helping himself to a chocolate biscuit when no one was watching.

"Bad stuff happens," sighed Dormouse.

They all bowed their heads as Badger said a prayer.

Then Mole, whose life was spent mostly in the dark, got up and said, "My heart is heavy. All creatures of The Great Forest must one day die; why, I do not know. Today it was Weasel's turn. Weasel told lots of fibs, but I shall miss him. My eyes are not good, as you all know. Weasel helped me find my way home whenever I got lost. I shall miss him very much."

"Weasel was kind," agreed Possum.

Rat (who hadn't been invited to the party) got up and said, "It is most regRATable that Weasel is no longer a member of this fRATernity. They say Weasel was sly. Well, maybe he was, but he was my friend. Weasel saved me once from Pit Bull's wRATh. Pit Bull was just about to snap my neck when Weasel bit his tail, and I fell to the ground and ran to safety. I will always be gRATeful to him."

"Weasel was brave and he was a good friend," Possum agreed.

Raccoon scratched his belly. "Weasel was my friend, too. He taught me all I know about stealing birds' eggs."

"Shame!" cried Robin.

"Weasel was my cousin," said Ferret. "He showed me the best places to find the most delicious bugs."

"Bugs are creatures of The Great Forest, too, you know!" yelled Earwig from a crack in the ceiling. His voice was so tiny that hardly anyone heard him.

"He shared with others," said Possum. "Weasel was generous."

"Weasel will be sadly missed," said Badger, echoing the feelings of everyone present. "Nannycatch Meadows will not be the same without him."

"Indeed, his death leaves an empty space in all our lives," said Possum.

"Not in mine!" yelled Earwig.

"Why must we die?" moaned Mole, shaking his head.

"I wish we knew the answer," said Badger. "We live and we die. That's all we know."

"Let us all drink a toast to Weasel," said Possum. "Please raise your glasses."

His friends raised their root beers.

"To kind, brave, generous Weasel," said Possum.

"To kind, brave, generous Weasel!" everyone cried.

"Now it's time for me to cut the cake," said Possum.

And that is what he did, and everyone had a jolly time, and it wasn't such a dreadful birthday party after all.

CHAPTER 2

CONCERNING ELEPHANTS

There are no elephants of any kind in The Great Forest.

FLIGHT FROM DANGER

Uncle Possum had consumed far too many chocolate biscuits, too much cake and way too many root beers at Possum's birthday party. Too ill to travel back home, he stayed the night in his nephew's spare room, clutching his stomach and groaning through most of the night.

The next morning, while Uncle Possum slept, Possum ate a small but nutritious breakfast and then set off on his usual walk along the pleasant trails of Nannycatch Meadows.

He hadn't gone far when his friend Pigeon alighted on a nearby branch. "TERRIBLE NEWS," he said, handing Possum his *Nannycatch News*.

Nannycatch News was published irregularly: sometimes it came out in the early morning, sometimes in the evening, and sometimes at midnight for nocturnals like

Moth, Owl and Bat. Sometimes, especially if there was no news, it didn't come out at all. Today, however, the headline was disturbing: "CHAOS AND PANIC IN THE GREAT FOREST!"

"Whatever has happened, Pigeon?"

Pigeon paced back and forth, nodding his head. "HUNDREDS OF CREATURES HOMELESS! CHAINSAWS AND BULLDOZERS TEAR DOWN TREES. ENORMOUS CRATERS IN SWINEBELLY BECK AND DANBY WISKE."

Swinebelly Beck and Danby Wiske lay at the northern edge of The Great Forest. Swinebelly Beck was named after the mountain stream, or beck, that emptied into Muddy Harbour. It bordered Cringle End. Together the three communities formed one of the prettiest areas in all of The Great Forest.

But now, according to Pigeon and the *Nannycatch News*, two of these communities were being destroyed to make way for a restaurant, a gift shop, a parking lot and an outdoor swimming pool.

"NEW HIGHWAY TO BLAME," said Pigeon angrily. "GREAT FOREST SHRINKING. HUNDREDS OF TERRIFIED CREATURES RUN FROM BULLDOZERS."

Possum thanked Pigeon and hurried back home to tell Uncle Possum the awful news, but Uncle was still in bed with his door closed.

Meanwhile, Chief Moose had declared a state of emergency. His cry for help was carried by Wind throughout

The Great Forest: "Take the homeless refugees into your homes and into your hearts!" sighed Wind.

I must help, Possum said to himself, as he listened to Wind's message.

Later, when Uncle Possum finally got up, he complained to his young nephew, "Your bed is not comfortable. It is much too soft. I hardly slept. I haven't the energy to walk home. I must stay with you a further night to recover my strength."

Possum said, "You know I am always delighted to have you, Uncle, but there is an emergency, and I'm afraid that you must leave."

Uncle Possum was indignant. "Emergency?"

"Yes, Uncle."

"Leave?"

"Yes, Uncle." He handed him the *Nannycatch News* so he could see for himself.

Uncle Possum glanced at the paper and threw it down. "Fiddlesticks!" he said angrily.

"My duty is to my unfortunate fellow creatures," said Possum.

"I have never heard of such a thing!" snarled Uncle Possum. "They are only unfortunate because they are lazy good-for-nothings. I am your uncle. You cannot order me to go. I refuse to leave."

"Oh, dear," sighed Possum. His uncle did not understand.

How could Possum ignore Chief Moose's plea for help? He simply couldn't. He looked around his comfortable little home, so tidy and safe in the great old oak, and wondered what to do. Then he had an idea: his uncle could stay, and he would sleep in his hammock high up in the leafy canopy of the oak tree. The nights were still too cold for sleeping outdoors, for it was not yet summer, but he could take extra blankets. He would manage somehow; after all, it was an emergency. He set off to see Chief Moose.

"I have room for one, Chief Moose," he said, "and I'm sure my friends will help also."

"Thank you, Possum," said Chief Moose. "I'm proud of you and your Nannycatch friends. The Great Forest would be a poorer place without you. I will arrange for the homeless Shrew family to make their way to your pretty Nannycatch home immediately. Shrews are small creatures and should fit quite nicely into one room."

The refugees arrived that same afternoon. Shrew said, "Thank you for your kind hospitality, Possum. It is most good-

hearted of you to take us in.
We are in your debt. I
hope we will not
be a burden; we
don't wish to
cause you any trouble."

"No trouble at all. You
were lucky to escape from Swinebelly Beck with your
lives. It is an honour to have you here in my humble
home. You are most welcome. We are all creatures of
The Great Forest and must help one another."

"Noble sentiments, indeed," said Shrew. "Thank you,
Possum."

"I will take your room, Nephew," said Uncle Possum.
"Perhaps the bed is a little more comfortable."

So Uncle Possum took his nephew's room; Shrew and
his family took the guest room; and Possum, carrying
two wool blankets, moved up to his hammock.

Arguments started during the very first night. They
were so loud that Possum could hear the noise from his
high hammock. Shrew complained to his wife of an
injury to his hind leg. The pain was keeping him awake.
"I must have pulled a muscle in our flight to freedom,"
he groaned.

"There is nothing whatever the matter with your leg,"
yelled Shrew's wife. "You are simply too lazy to go out
and find a new place for your family."

"Aargh!" groaned Shrew. "I am in great pain."

"Lazy good-for-nothing!" yelled his wife.

Shrew's eleven children started crying and shrieking.

"Now look what you've done!" screamed Shrew's wife.

"It's your job to keep them quiet!" yelled Shrew over the noise.

The children shrieked even louder.

Uncle Possum came bursting into their room. He was angry. "What is all this noise? I am old and I need my sleep!"

Possum, high up in his oak-tree hammock, covered his ears with blankets to escape the noise of their quarrelling. But it was no good. They continued to scream at one another. The din was frightful. Possum had a poor night's sleep.

The next morning the same arguments started again at breakfast. "Ah! The terrible pain in my leg!" cried Shrew.

"There's nothing wrong with your leg!" yelled his wife.

The children's screams brought Uncle Possum, not yet quite awake, stumbling from his room. "Let me see that leg of yours," he demanded. "Lie on the floor. I will fix it for you. And then I might get some proper sleep."

Possum crawled out of his hammock, climbed down the oak tree and watched through the window, as his uncle wrestled with Shrew's leg. "Not that one!" cried Shrew. "It's the other leg." Uncle Possum turned and attacked the other leg, twisting and turning, pressing and pulling, until Shrew finally screamed, "My back! You've broken my back!"

"You monster!" screamed Shrew's wife, grabbing a frying pan and attacking Uncle Possum. "How dare you break my poor husband's back!"

"Monster! Monster!" screamed the kids, leaping onto Uncle Possum and beating him with their tiny paws. Uncle Possum threw them all off, retreated to his room and slammed the door.

Oh, dear! I think I will go and stay with my friend Raccoon for a while, until this emergency is over. I'll return in a day or two, Possum said to himself, *when everyone has gone.*

Raccoon's home, in a tall cedar tree, was large and comfortable. Raccoon was delighted to see his friend. "Stay as long as you like, Possum. Gopher and his family fled from the cruel bulldozers at Danby Wiske and stayed last night. They moved out this morning to build a new home over in Sheepshank Knott."

"Sheepshank Knott is a pleasant place," said Possum. "What a pity about Swinebelly Beck and Danby Wiske, though."

Raccoon sat up and scratched his belly. "Yes, indeed. May the Spirit of The Great Forest keep Nannycatch Meadows safe from the deadly bulldozers."

Possum stayed with Raccoon for two pleasant days but missed his own cosy little home. "Uncle Possum and Shrew should be gone by now," he said to Raccoon. "I shall take my leave. Thank you for your kind hospitality."

"Not at all, Possum. It was a pleasure to have you stay."

When Possum got back to his home it was empty. Shrew and his family had moved on, and there was no sign of his uncle. "Phew!" Possum sighed with relief.

Shrew had left a thank-you note: *You will always be our friend, Possum*. It was signed, *Shrew*.

Possum decided to celebrate his return with ice cream. He looked in his freezer, but it was empty: there was no ice cream, not even a lick. He opened his fridge, but it was also empty: there wasn't even a carrot left in the crisper. He peered into his biscuit jar, but not a crumb remained. He checked his nut cupboard, but it was bare: not a walnut or an acorn was left. He inspected his tea caddy, but not one tea-bag had survived.

The reason everyone had moved out, Possum realized, was because they had eaten everything. "Oh, well," he sighed. "At least I helped Shrew in his time of need."

He climbed up onto his roof. Robin flew down to join him. "I hear you took care of Shrew and his family. That was good of you."

"I did what I could," said Possum. "What about you?"

Robin flicked her tail. "I had Magpie stay a couple of days. She left this morning. Did you hear about Ferret?"

"Ferret? No."

"He took Earwig and his family into his home—forty-eight young ones, exhausted after their escape from the cruel bulldozers at Swinebelly Beck, poor things, and they had to wait in the Foggy Bottom Refugee Camp with no food or water. Chief Moose handed them over to Ferret, and as soon as the Chief left, Ferret had Earwig and his family for lunch."

"Ferret is a very generous host," said Possum.

"Very hungry host, more like," said Robin. "He lunched on stir-fried earwigs."

Possum was horrified. "You mean he—?"

Robin nodded. "Every last one of them," she said, trying hard not to cry.

"I must go back inside," said Possum. "I feel ill. Perhaps a cup of tea—" But then he remembered that his tea caddy was empty. *I will visit my friend Chipmunk,* he said to himself. *He never runs out of tea.*

He said goodbye to Robin and hurried over to Chipmunk's snug home inside a stout hemlock tree. "I dropped in for a visit," he said to Chipmunk. "I'm afraid I've run out of tea."

"Welcome, Possum," said Chipmunk. "But you look frightfully pale. I'll put on the kettle right away."

"Thank you," said Possum, sinking into Chipmunk's comfortable couch. "The world always seems brighter after a cup of tea."

"It does, indeed," said Chipmunk, "especially with some hot buttered scones and jam."

"You are such a good, dependable friend, Chipmunk," said Possum with a grateful sigh.

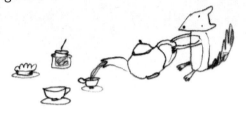

CHAPTER 4

RAIN

What a morning!

Possum peered out the window of his comfortable little oak-tree home at Rain and Wind playing together in the meadow. They pounded on Possum's windows and chased each other, Rain singing and dancing in the puddles, Wind tossing the trees and whistling and cavorting in Possum's chimney.

Possum shivered. There would be no early morning walk along Nannycatch trails for him today. It was a day for staying at home. He lit a crackling fire in the grate and then sat down to write a letter to Uncle Possum in Grotty Bottom.

Dear Uncle,

I hope you have forgiven your unworthy nephew for taking in the Shrew family and thus causing you some inconvenience, but sometimes (now that you have had some time to reflect, I'm sure you will agree) a Possum's duty as a member of our Great Forest community comes before the small comforts of family life, especially in times of emergency when our fellow creatures are suffering.

Please come and visit me again soon. There is sure to be some of your favourite rhubarb pie and ice cream waiting for you. And I have a new green tea about which I am anxious to get your opinion.

Your loving nephew,

Possum

He put down his pen, peered out the window at the weather once again and spotted his friend Chipmunk bent over by the force of Wind as he jogged through the storm. Chipmunk never missed his morning exercise, no matter whether the weather was warm and wonderful or whether the weather was wet and windy. Possum admired him for that. He wished he were as strong and fit as Chipmunk. *I will start exercising*, Possum said to himself. *Soon, but not today: it is far too cold and wet. Tomorrow for certain.*

He stayed watching at the window until Chipmunk, jogging through puddles and up and down the trunks of trees, had moved on out of sight. Then Possum addressed an envelope, carefully folded his Uncle Possum's letter, slid it inside the envelope, licked and sealed the flap and propped the letter up on the mantel for Pigeon—who was unlikely to let the storm keep him from his appointed rounds—to pick up later in the day. Then he made himself a cup of tea and sat beside his fire reading an exciting wolf story called *White Fang* until it was time for his morning nap.

By the next day the storm had passed. Possum was just about to set off on his morning walk when Pigeon made a perfect landing right outside his front door. "LETTER FROM UNCLE POSSUM," he said.

"My, that was quick." Possum opened the envelope and took out its single page.

Dear Nephew,

No, I have not forgiven you. Shrew accused me of breaking his back, when I was merely trying to help the ungrateful old fool! I left that very afternoon, resolving never to speak to any member of that family ever again. On my way out the door, I accidentally dropped my suitcase. The very loud thump scared Shrew's eleven little ones out of their tiny little minds. Ha! Serves the cheeky brats right.

I shall be glad to stop by for some of that rhubarb pie and ice cream you mention, and will be pleased to offer an opinion on your green tea.

Your unforgiving,

Uncle Possum

Possum folded the letter and slipped it back in its envelope.

"BAD NEWS?" asked Pigeon.

"Not really," said Possum with a grin. "But Shrew and his family are not likely to be inviting Uncle Possum into their new home any time soon."

CHAPTER 5

UNCLE POSSUM'S HEART OPERATION

Possum was resting in his hammock on the roof of his little home when Pigeon landed beside him in a flutter of wings. "READ ALL ABOUT IT," he said.

Possum glanced at the headline of his *Nannycatch News*: "REFUGEES FIND NEW HOMES BUT MANY MISSING OR DEAD." Then there followed a couple of paragraphs about Chief Moose's comments and his thanks to the creatures of The Great Forest for coming to the aid of the refugees.

Chipmunk scrambled onto Possum's hammock. "Say, isn't that your Grotty Bottom uncle down below in your front yard, reading in the sunshine?"

"It is, indeed," said Possum. "My dear uncle will be staying with me while he has his operation."

As Possum, Chipmunk and Pigeon looked down, they noticed Skunk eating Uncle Possum's breakfast scraps on the grass.

"Begone, scrounger!" Uncle Possum shouted angrily, hurling his book at Skunk and flattening him. "I hate bums!"

"UNCLE KILLS SKUNK!" screeched Pigeon, flapping his wings in alarm.

"Oh dear! It was an accident," said Possum. "A mishap. I'm sure Uncle meant Skunk no harm."

"MOST UPSETTING," said Pigeon.

"I saw that!" said Squirrel, hopping onto Possum's roof. "I never liked Skunk's body odour much, but he had a right to live his life, same as everyone else. Your uncle had no right to kill the little stinker."

Chipmunk said, "Your uncle has a nasty temper, Possum."

Possum sighed. "Yes, I know."

"I'm most upset," said Robin, gliding down from under the leaves where she had been leaves-dropping. "Since your uncle showed up in Nannycatch Meadows, bad things have been happening. We have to do something about him. Maybe we should speak to Chief Moose."

"That won't be necessary," said Possum. "Uncle is having his operation tomorrow morning."

"What kind of operation?" asked Chipmunk.

Possum said, "It's his heart."

"Your uncle has a weak heart?" asked Squirrel.

"Not weak, just nasty," said Possum. "You saw what happened to Skunk. Uncle's heart grows nastier and meaner every year. He yells at babies, he doesn't believe in Christmas or coloured crayons or bubblegum, and he never plays any games. Uncle Possum doesn't even know the meaning of fun. An operation is his only hope of becoming kinder and gentler. If the operation cures him, then we won't need advice from Chief Moose."

That same evening everyone attended Skunk's funeral. He was buried near Barbeck Tarn (a tarn is a mountain lake) under the green skunk cabbages he loved so much. Forget-me-not seeds were planted nearby, and a small monument was erect-ed—a white pine pole  with Skunk's name carved by Woodpecker.

Badger conducted the service, and many came forward to say a few kind words about Skunk.

"Poor Skunk," said Ferret. "He was a lovable old rogue. I shall miss him."

"I wish I could understand it," said Mole.

"Understand what?" asked Badger.

"Why we must die," answered Mole sadly, shaking his head and turning his blind eyes up to the sky.

"Search me," said Chipmunk. "Death is a mystery."

"I do not know the answer," said Badger, shaking his head and comforting Mole with gentle pats to the shoulder.

"Bad stuff happens," said Dormouse with a shrug.

"At least it was quick," said Ferret.

"I liked Skunk," said Chipmunk. "He was a good critter."

"Why, why, why?" cried Mole again.

"Search me," said Chipmunk once more.

Badger just shook his head.

"There's nothing much any of us can do," said Robin, wiping away a tear.

. . .

Uncle Possum suffered no complications from his operation. Even though his heart was nasty and mean, it was extremely strong.

Moaning and groaning, he rested in Possum's warm and comfortable home while Possum took care of his every need, feeding him the juiciest grubs and maggots for breakfast every morning, the most tender caterpillars and mosquito larvae for lunch and the most delicious ladybird and lacewing soup for dinner.

"If the operation is a success, perhaps your uncle will become a vegetarian like us," Chipmunk said to an exhausted Possum one afternoon, as he rested on the bank of the tiny beck that burbled gently beside his home. "If everyone ate nuts and greens, there would be no need to harm living creatures."

Possum said, "I made Uncle a stack of my dandelion pancakes this morning, but he threw them out the window. They landed on Mole and covered him in butter and syrup."

"Poor critter," said Chipmunk. "What did your uncle do?"

"Nothing. He just laughed."

"Doesn't look like the operation is working," said Chipmunk.

"Not yet," agreed Possum sadly. "Perhaps it takes time."

But after another week, Uncle's heart was still nasty. "My bed is too lumpy," he complained to Possum, "and the house is freezing."

The next day he grumbled about the sameness of the food, even though Possum was doing his best to feed him a variety of tasty dishes and keep him comfortable and warm.

The operation had failed, Possum decided.

"When that plate of pancakes hit me, I was sticky for a week," Mole later told Possum. "But I'm not complaining: I'm lucky to be alive."

It wasn't long before Possum was thin and pale from worry, hard work and lack of sleep. Just when he didn't think he could take any more, Uncle Possum decided to leave. "I've had enough of this cold, draughty place!" he complained. "I'm going home to my cottage in Grotty Bottom."

Possum's friends turned out to see his uncle go. Besides Chipmunk, Robin, Squirrel and Raccoon, there were Deer and Brown Bear, Stoat and Otter, Ferret and Toad, Coyote and Fox, Beaver and Pigeon and many others, including Mole, still a little sticky from the pancake syrup. They crowded together in Possum's front yard. "Have a safe and pleasant journey," they called, as Possum's uncle grabbed his suitcase.

"Out of my way!" he snarled at them.

Possum opened the gate for him. "Goodbye, Uncle. Come again soon."

"A hundred years from now would be too soon," growled his uncle.

Possum watched Uncle heading toward the main forest path. Hare popped his head out of his burrow to see what all the commotion was about.

"Out of my way!" growled Uncle, walloping a chestnut tree with his walking-stick. The blow was so hard that it caused a rotten limb to fall down and strike Hare on the head. Hare flopped over and lay still.

Uncle Possum didn't even notice. He kept going without a backward glance.

"MOST UPSETTING," said Pigeon, as everyone rushed to Hare's side.

"Hare today, gone tomorrow," said Hawk, dropping from the sky like a stone.

"That's not very kind, Hawk," said Raccoon.

Hawk hung his head, ashamed. "Sorry."

"This is dreadful," cried Robin, wiping away a tear. "Never again will Hare nibble sweet skunk cabbage or purple vetch; never again will he hippity-hop through fields of scented clover or chase butterflies through the long grass; never again—"

"Hold on!" said Raccoon. "Hare's not dead!"

Raccoon was right. Hare stirred and opened his eyes. "Oh! My head!" he groaned.

Everyone cheered. "Hare is alive!" they shouted.

• • •

The next morning, Possum was lying in his hammock when Pigeon landed beside him in a confusion of white wings.

"YOUR MORNING PAPER, POSSUM," said Pigeon, dropping it into the hammock. "PICTURE OF BANDAGED HARE, FRONT PAGE. HARE IN HOSPITAL AT LEAST A MONTH."

"Poor Hare," said Possum. "It was an accident. My uncle meant no harm. We'll all miss him."

"Miss your uncle?" asked Pigeon, forgetting to talk in headlines.

"No, miss Hare while he is in hospital," said Possum.

Robin flew down and perched on a branch above Possum's head. "It must be quiet now with your uncle gone."

Possum sighed contentedly. "You can say that again."

"It must be quiet now with your uncle gone," Robin said again.

Possum closed his eyes. The sun was warm on his face. Life was good. He had his snug little home, and he had friends like Chipmunk and Robin and Pigeon and all the others.

Robin said, "It's just too bad your uncle's heart operation wasn't successful."

"The most difficult thing of all to fix," Possum murmured, "is a heart."

CHAPTER 6

SCHOOL

ossum liked to be wakened early by the sun pouring through the window of his little home in the old oak tree. But this morning somebody was chattering excitedly outside his door before the sun had even reached his window.

He scrambled out of bed and hurried to the door. It was Robin. "What's up?" asked Possum, rubbing sleep from his eyes.

"Possum, I think you had better get over to Nannycatch School right away!"

"Why, Robin? What's happening?"

"Brown Bear, the regular teacher, is off sick. Your uncle volunteered to substitute teach."

"Oh, dear! I'd better get over there as fast as I can. I would hate Uncle to be nasty to the children. Thank you, Robin."

He checked the time. School would be starting in a few minutes. He would have to be quick. Without stopping to cook breakfast for himself or even make a cup of tea, Possum hurried off to the school.

Nannycatch School lay in a pretty little clearing at the edge of a meadow with a tinkling beck flowing through it. About fifty kits, pups and fledglings, a mixture of young ferrets, squirrels, raccoons, ducks, moles, beavers, swallows, blackbirds and other creatures, including one tiny ladder-backed woodpecker, were standing around listening to their substitute teacher, Uncle Possum.

Possum sat at the edge of the beck, watching and listening. If Uncle said or did anything nasty, he would try to intervene and help out. He watched Uncle Possum split the students into groups so that all ducks were together, all squirrels, all blackbirds, and so on. "Good," said Uncle Possum. "Now each group will begin working on its skills." He clapped his paws. "Off you go."

Possum watched as young squirrels started practising their rapid tree climbing, ducks their deep diving and speedy swimming, swallows their extra-low swooping and flycatching, tiny woodpecker her rapid rat-a-tat on a rowan tree, and so on, each creature practising skills suited to its nature.

"No! No! No!" cried Uncle Possum. "Come back here at once!"

The bewildered creatures stopped what they were doing and gathered once more around their substitute teacher.

"You are wasting time, all of you," said Uncle Possum. "You young swallows are already adept at low swooping and flycatching; ducks, you are fairly proficient at deep diving and speedy swimming. So why do you all waste time practising skills you already have? The purpose of school, children, is to take courses in the things you do not know. So my task as teacher is to help you learn extra skills, skills you do not have. Ducks, therefore, will take my course in Tree Climbing, squirrels and swallows will take my course in Swimming, blackbirds and beavers will take Tunnel Burrowing, and so on. Moles, rabbits and ferrets must build up their leg and arm muscles so they can take Flying. Raccoons and skunks will work on Basic Tree Gnawing & Dam Building. Get the idea?"

A scrawny raccoon kit spoke up. "But raccoons and skunks don't gnaw trees and build dams. Only beavers do that."

"That's right," said a plump little blackbird. "We fly. We don't burrow tunnels like moles."

"Then it's time you learned," snapped Uncle Possum, clapping his paws once again. In his loudest voice he said, "Form groups, and practise your new skills."

Possum watched as the little ones began their various courses. Squirrels and swallows jumped into the beck, squirming frantically to stay afloat, wings and paws shooting out in all directions. Ducks took turns attacking the bark of a thin birch tree with their webbed feet as they attempted to climb. They failed dismally, falling to the ground moaning in agony. Moles, rabbits and ferrets leaped up and down flapping their arms, trying to fly. Raccoons and skunks gnawed a stout fir tree, breaking their teeth and falling back in great pain. "Ouch!" they cried as they rubbed their bleeding gums.

Possum couldn't believe his eyes. He turned his attention back to the young squirrels and swallows that were now standing in a circle on the bank of the beck. In the middle of the circle lay a drowned swallow. The young ladder-backed woodpecker, who had joined the swallows at swimming, was frantically trying to revive her.

"Is she drowned?" asked Possum.

"I think so. Swallow swallowed a lot of water," said the ladder-backed woodpecker, trying hard to breathe air into the swallow's tiny lungs.

Possum bent over the unfortunate swallow. The young flycatcher's wings and breast were still.

"She's quite dead," sighed the ladder-backed woodpecker at last.

Just then a cry came from the opposite side of the clearing. A young rabbit, believing he was ready to fly, had launched himself into the air from the top of a cedar tree, flapping his ears and arms wildly and yelling, "Look at me! I'm flying! Look at me!" But he wasn't flying: he fell to the ground and broke his tailbone.

His friends rushed over to help him up.

Possum scratched his head. His uncle's theory seemed flawed. If they practised for the rest of their lives, would squirrels and swallows ever make good swimmers? And were the teeth of raccoons and skunks big and strong enough to gnaw trees and build dams? Could blackbirds and beavers ever learn to burrow under the ground like moles and rabbits? Would ducks ever win medals at climbing trees? And wasn't the notion of moles, rabbits and ferrets learning to fly quite absurd? Had Nature designed them for these tasks?

"One of your students is dead, Uncle," said Possum, "and a young rabbit is lucky to be alive. This kind of work is too hard for you at your great age, Uncle—teaching, I mean. You must give it up."

"There is bound to be the occasional accident," Uncle Possum admitted, slashing the air with his cane and just missing a young hummingbird hovering above his head. "But you're quite right, Nephew," said Uncle Possum.

"Perhaps it's time for me to retire from substitute teaching. Besides, I have a headache from all the noise. I'm going home and back to bed."

And off he went.

The students began to gather around Possum. "That will be all for today, children," said Possum. "Class is dismissed."

"Wheee!" cried the beavers, ferrets and raccoons.

"Pip-pip," squeaked the blackbirds.

"Yippee-quack!" yelled the ducks.

"Gee, thanks, Possum," said the squirrels and swallows.

"We will stay and help you bury young swallow," said the young moles and rabbits.

After the burial, Possum headed for home, still thinking about his uncle's theory of education. *Might as well try to teach a tree to boil a kettle and make a cup of tea,* he thought, which reminded him that he had not yet had his morning cup of tea. He hurried home all the faster.

That evening, Robin dropped in. Possum was swinging in his hammock. "How was your uncle's teaching at Nannycatch School today?" asked Robin, tongue in beak.

Possum said, "He's a rotten teacher, Robin. I asked him to give it up. Teaching kids is a special talent, one that takes plenty of heart."

Robin flicked her tail. "Which Uncle Possum hasn't got."

"Here comes Chipmunk," said Possum. "I'll go down and put on the kettle. Would you care to join us for tea?"

CHAPTER 7

THE GREAT FOREST PROVIDES

Possum loved The Great Forest. He loved it in all its seasons, whether hushed and white with snow or aflame with the yellows and reds of autumn leaves. But best of all he loved it now, in the spring, as it burst boisterously, joyously forth with new green life.

Uncle Possum, having forgiven his outspoken and excitable nephew for their past misunderstandings and disagreements, had consented to join Possum and his new friend Hedgehog for a stroll through Nannycatch Meadows on this fine spring morning.

They sauntered past a busy ant colony, one that had been growing under the bracken through many generations of hard-working ants. Possum remembered the colony when it was a mere bump, and now it had grown to be a small hillock. He sometimes sat and watched the ants, fascinated by their energy and industry. He admired his busy neighbours very much.

The three walkers made their way toward Cringle End, Uncle Possum puffing on his cigar as he lectured his two young companions. "The Great Forest provides for us all," he said. "As a teacher, I have always tried to instil in my young students two important principles: one is the interdependence of all living things; the other is a respect for Nature. How do we show this respect? We show this respect by simply obeying Nature's laws. For example, we always leave a place as pristine and unpolluted as we find it."

He tossed his cigar stump over his shoulder, and it landed in the bracken. They walked on. They did not see Uncle Possum's cigar stub smoulder in the bracken. They did not see the bracken burst into flames and the Nannycatch ant colony quickly become a raging inferno. The fire soon burned itself out, but not before the ants were all burned to a crisp. The colony was no more. Not a single ant survived.

Meanwhile, the three walkers continued on their way.

"Here comes Chief Moose," said Possum.

Uncle Possum said, "Good morning, Chief. I was telling my nephew and Hedgehog here how The Great Forest provides for all our needs."

"Yes, indeed," said Chief Moose. "Come with me. I want to show you something."

They followed Chief Moose. After a while he halted and pointed to a huge red cedar tree, which had stood in Cringle End for centuries. "Read what is written at the foot of the tree," he said to Hedgehog.

Hedgehog read aloud the motto carved into the ancient cedar: "The Great Forest Will Provide."

"You are a good reader," said Chief Moose.

"I know," said Hedgehog, "but what does it mean, exactly?"

"It simply means," said Chief Moose, "that The Great Forest provides food and water and shelter and almost everything its creatures need."

"Why *almost* everything?" asked Possum. "What else could the crea- tures of The Great Forest possibly need besides plen- tiful food, clean water and safe shelter?"

Chief Moose smiled. "What else, Possum? There are four other needs. First comes Love. Everyone needs Love, or affec- tion and belonging."

"Love," agreed Uncle Possum, nodding his head wisely, though the only person he loved was himself.

"And then, after Love," continued Chief Moose, "every creature needs Freedom. Then comes Fun."

Uncle Possum continued nodding. "Freedom and Fun," he repeated, not fully understanding what the Chief meant by fun because he seldom had any.

"Finally," said Chief Moose, "all creatures need Success, or achievement."

"Quite right," said Uncle Possum, whose only achievement was the extra weight he carried around his tummy.

"These things," the Chief concluded, "Love, Freedom, Fun and Success, our Great Forest cannot provide. All its creatures must seek and find these for themselves."

"For themselves," echoed Uncle Possum, nodding in agreement.

Possum and Hedgehog thanked Chief Moose for his interesting observations on the needs of all Great Forest creatures, and the three walkers returned to Nanny-catch. "My friends Chipmunk and Robin are coming to tea," Possum told his uncle and Hedgehog. "Would you care to join us?"

"Tea and friendship," said Hedgehog. "What could be more delightful?"

"I must return to Grotty Bottom," said Uncle Possum. "It is time for my nap."

And that is what they did: Uncle Possum went home for his nap, while Hedgehog, Chipmunk, Robin and Possum sat down to tea in Possum's front yard with hot buttered scones and jam. To begin the conversation, Possum mentioned Chief Moose's interesting talk in the woods at Cringle End.

"Success," said Hedgehog. "What does that mean, exactly?"

"Search me," said Chipmunk.

They all had a jolly time discussing the meaning of Success, as well as the other important needs: Love, Freedom and Fun.

The next morning, Pigeon alighted on a branch above Possum's front door with the *Nannycatch News*. Possum opened his door and reached up for his copy. The headlines leaped out at him: "NANNYCATCH ANT COLONY DESTROYED BY FIRE."

"THOUSANDS OF ANTS DIE," said Pigeon.

Possum was shocked. "Oh, dear! What a terrible calamity! How could such a thing happen?"

"CIGARETTE SUSPECTED," said Pigeon.

Possum thought for a moment. "Or a cigar stub," he murmured to himself.

Chapter 8

Gallantry and Heroism

ossum enjoyed reading. It was fun. He especially liked to read adventure stories of gallantry and heroism.

During the winter he read in the warmth and comfort of his cosy little home in the old oak tree, feet propped up near the fire. But as soon as spring arrived, he carried his books up to his hammock, where he could read, keep an eye on the activity in Nannycatch Meadows and see the sea sparkling in the far distance.

"I wish I were a hero," he said to his friend Chipmunk one morning, as he rocked slowly in his hammock. "The problem with Nannycatch Meadows is that it is just a little too quiet and peaceful."

"You can't be serious," said Chipmunk, scampering up onto the end of Possum's hammock, so he could rock along with his friend as they talked. "Listen to Crow up in the high branches. He makes almost as much noise as a chainsaw in Danby Wiske."

"What I mean is, nothing exciting ever happens here," said Possum. "How can I ever be a hero if nothing exciting ever happens?"

Chipmunk shrugged. "Search me."

"There's no dragon for me to slay, no magic ring for me to find, no helpless maid to rescue from evil, no dangerous quest, nothing. How can I ever be a hero like the ones in the books?"

Chipmunk said, "Here comes Chief Moose. Why not ask him?"

"Good morning, gentlemen," said Chief Moose. "What's your problem?"

"No problem, Chief Moose," said Chipmunk. "It's just that Possum would like to be a hero, but nothing much ever happens in Nannycatch Meadows."

"I know what you mean," said Chief Moose, scratching his antlers on an overhanging bough. "The Great

Forest is mostly peaceful and quiet, all right, and that's the way I like it."

"But what do I do, Chief?" asked Possum. "How can I be a hero if nothing exciting ever happens?"

"Be happy," said the Chief. "Keep reading, keep rocking in your hammock, enjoy your freedom and the affection of your friends, achieve inner peace, have fun, help others whenever you can."

"That's it?" said Possum.

"That's it," said the Chief.

"Never mind about being a hero?" said Possum.

"You got it," said the Chief.

"Uh, thanks, Chief," said Possum doubtfully.

"Don't mention it. See you boys around."

"Keep rocking?" said Possum to Chipmunk when Chief Moose had gone.

"That's what he said," said Chipmunk. "Keep reading. Keep rocking. Be happy. Have fun. Help others."

"OK," said Possum, "let's go get our friends Ferret and Squirrel and help them take a fun swim in Snottynose Pool."

"Race you there!" said Chipmunk.

CHAPTER 9

A HORRIFYING STORY

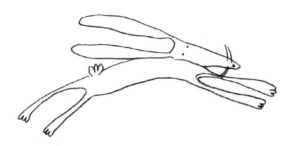

The land adjoining Dollywaggon Bottom is riddled with ancient burrows, most of them collapsed and in ruins and no longer used, except by the Rattlesnake family.

Rabbit's youngest, Bunny, was lost in one of the old burrows, and she was fearful for her child's safety. She asked a neighbour to watch her other little ones while she searched for her missing baby.

So efficient was communication in The Great Forest—Wind to trees, trees to birds, birds to grass—that soon everyone knew of tiny Bunny's plight.

Rescue teams under the leadership of Chief Moose rushed to the scene. Possum and Chipmunk volunteered to search Crackpot Edge, a maze of burrows on Dollywaggon Bottom's northern border. Possum headed in with flashlight and shovel; Chipmunk followed with water bottles and ropes. They couldn't call out, for the smallest quiver could send the roof down on top of them and bury them alive.

They searched the narrow tunnels for hours. Sometimes a tunnel came to an end where its roof had collapsed, blocking the way ahead, and they had to turn and make their way back and try a different entrance. Once or twice they ran into unfriendly rattlesnakes that hissed at them and showed their fangs. The two searchers were tired and just about ready to give up when Chipmunk said, "Listen!"

Possum listened but could hear nothing; the burrow was as dark and silent as Mole's basement. Then he heard a faint squeak.

"This way!" said Chipmunk, setting off down a branch of the tunnel. Possum followed, only to come to a dead end—another collapsed roof. A second squeak came, louder this time. Chipmunk got busy with the shovel while Possum held the flashlight. When Chipmunk tired, Possum took over. Soon they were through to the other side. Baby Bunny was waiting for them. She was not jumping with excitement, because of a broken leg, but she did squeak happily at the sight of Possum and Chipmunk's friendly faces.

Possum carried Bunny on his shoulders all the way back to the burrow entrance in less time than it takes a pair of crows to start an argument.

Rabbit, happy at the sight of her lost baby, broke down and wept with relief and joy. Then she gave Possum and Chipmunk a humongous hug, thanking them.

The next morning, Pigeon landed on Possum's roof with the *Nannycatch News*. "POSSUM AND CHIPMUNK SAVE BUNNY," said the headlines. "YOU ARE HEROES," said Pigeon. "PICTURES ON FRONT PAGE."

"We were only doing our duty," said Possum modestly.

A week later, Possum discovered a small news item on the back page of his morning paper:

BABY BUNNY'S NARROW ESCAPE

Eagle snatched Baby Bunny from outside her burrow yesterday afternoon but did not get very far: Robin saw the bold attack and rushed to the rescue, pecking bravely at Eagle until he was forced to release his prey. Bunny fell a short distance to the ground and was not hurt. This is Bunny's second incident in a week: she was rescued by Possum and Chipmunk last Monday from the dangerous Dollywaggon Bottom burrows. Chief Moose said, "Robin deserves a medal for heroism."

Robin flew down and perched on Possum's hammock. "Robin, you're a hero!" said Possum. "You saved Bunny. I'm proud of you."

Robin, embarrassed, blushed scarlet all over. Then she flicked her tail. "I'm not just a pretty face, you know."

CHAPTER 10

A MOST PECULIAR RACE

Possum's aquatic friends were holding their annual water race in the cool waters of Swinebelly Beck at the spot where it flowed through a green glade at the edge of Biskey Fen. Uncle Possum came up from Grotty Bottom to judge the event, though he hadn't been asked.

But Lynx had already been appointed judge. Uncle Possum was quite annoyed; wasn't he a Great Forest Elder? Lynx was a nobody, in his opinion.

The seven competitors were Toad, Turtle, Frog, Newt, Salamander, Watersnake and Crayfish.

"What about you, Otter?" asked Lynx. "Are you not competing this year?"

"No, thanks," said Otter. "I won last year, remember? Someone else should have a chance at winning."

"That's very sporting of you," said Lynx. He turned to the assembled crowd. "Last call for competitors."

To many of the animals' surprise, a creature that looked a lot like Weasel stepped forward. "I, too, wish to be in the race," he said.

"But I thought Weasel was flattened on the highway," Possum whispered to his friends. "Remember? It was the day of my birthday party."

"I remember," said Chipmunk.

"He was quite dead," said Ferret.

"This is Weasel's father," explained Robin. "It is Weasel Senior who wishes to enter the Great Annual Water Race."

"Weasel Senior is much too old," said Raccoon.

"And not quite right in the head," pointed out Chipmunk.

"And he's not aquatic," said Ferret. "Weasels are not great swimmers. The other competitors are water dwellers, but Weasel is a denizen of the forest, like us."

Uncle Possum stepped forward and stood beside Weasel Senior. "Old Weasel has as much right to be in the race as anyone else," he declared. He turned to Lynx. "Unless you wish to be sued for unlawful discrimination, then Weasel must be allowed to race, the same as the others."

Hedgehog scratched his head. "Unlawful discrimination. What does that mean, exactly?"

"Search me," said Chipmunk.

"I, too, am not quite sure what unlawful discrimination means," admitted Lynx. "But I do know that if Weasel

Senior attempts to race with aquatic competitors, he stands very little chance of winning. Not only that, but he runs the risk of injury, and even death."

"Death? Did you say death?" Weasel Senior took two steps backward. His face was pale. "Perhaps I was a little hasty."

Uncle Possum pushed him forward. "All creatures are equal under the law. Old Weasel has as much right to be in the race as Frog or Toad or anyone."

Weasel Senior squirmed. "Yes, but..."

Uncle Possum was stern. "You cannot change your mind now, not after I have fought so hard for your rights. You will race, and that's the end of it."

"Yes, but..." said Weasel Senior.

"Be quiet," snapped Uncle Possum. "You have said enough."

"Very well," said Lynx. "Old Weasel may race if that is his wish."

Lynx gave the signal for the race to start. The eight athletes dived into the water and began swimming vigorously upstream toward the finish a hundred metres away.

Possum, Chipmunk and Ferret followed Lynx, running along the bank of the beck in front of the cheering spectators.

Toad leaped out onto the bank and began hopping furiously toward the finish.

"Toad is cheating!" screamed Ferret.

"Cheating is allowed," said Lynx calmly, "unless you get caught. Then it is not allowed, unless you have a good excuse."

Frog also cheated, leaping along, using rocks as stepping-stones. He soon drew level with Toad and tripped him.

"Foul!" cried Chipmunk.

"Bodychecking is allowed," said Lynx.

The race continued.

Weasel Senior, frightened that he might drown, hung onto Watersnake's tail.

Salamander got a cramp and quit after only twenty-five metres.

Newt, chasing after a bright dragon-fly, was swept downstream and out of the race.

Crayfish spotted a shapely set of antennae waving at him from under a submerged rock. He swam down to investigate and forgot about the race.

"Disqualified!" yelled Lynx.

Weasel managed to make it to the half-way mark before slipping off Watersnake's tail and plunging to the bottom.

"Save old Weasel!" Chipmunk cried.

Except for Raccoon, who was busy scratching his belly, Possum's friends were not good swimmers. Nor, for that matter, was Possum, but without any hesitation he dived into the cold water and grasped Weasel Senior by the neck. After struggling for several minutes against the current, he managed to drag him to the bank, and then he collapsed, exhausted.

"Well done, Possum!" cried Lynx, as he and Ferret took turns applying mouth-to-mouth resuscitation. "Your heroic deed saved old Weasel."

Sure enough, Weasel Senior came to, coughing and spluttering.

As far as the race was concerned, Turtle had beaten Watersnake by a neck.

"Weasel Senior held me back by hanging on to my tail," complained Watersnake. "I should be declared winner."

"How can you talk of winning," said Lynx, "when poor old Weasel Senior nearly drowned?"

"Quite right," said Frog, who had finished third, narrowly beating Toad, who never did recover from being tripped up by Frog.

At The Great Forest Water Race prize-giving ceremony, Lynx hung a gold medal on a blue ribbon around Possum's neck for his brave rescue of Weasel Senior.

"A true hero!" cheered Turtle. Everyone applauded loudly.

"How wonderful!" exclaimed Robin, wiping away a tear of joy.

"MOST UPLIFTING," said Pigeon.

"And I declare Turtle the winner of The Great Forest Water Race!" shouted Lynx over the cheers of the crowd.

"Hooray!" they cried.

Watersnake was sulking. "It's not fair," he grumbled. "I should have won."

"What a peculiar race," Chipmunk said to Possum, as they made their way back to Nannycatch Meadows.

When they reached Possum's door, Possum said, "Will you come in for some tea?"

"Thank you," said Chipmunk. "There's nothing quite like a nice cup of tea to help make sense of everything. Have you any scones?"

"Of course."

"With jam?"

Possum smiled. "Just sit and relax while I put on the kettle."

They were still sitting and talking and drinking tea an hour later when Pigeon alighted on the window sill with an evening edition of the *Nannycatch News*.

Possum got up and went to the window.

There was a picture of Weasel Senior on the front page. "RACE CONTESTANT ALMOST DROWNS! POSSUM SAVES WEASEL SENIOR!" exclaimed the headlines.

Robin flew in through the open window, over Pigeon's head, and made a graceful landing onto the top of the teapot, one of the warmest spots in the house. "You were so brave, Possum," she said proudly, flicking her tail.

Possum shrugged modestly. "I'll make a fresh pot of tea for you, Robin, if you wouldn't mind getting off the pot."

CHAPTER 11

QUESTIONS FOR CHIEF MOOSE

P ossum was putting on the kettle for his morning tea
when there was a knock on his door.

"Who is it?" called Possum.

"It's me, Chief Moose," said Chief Moose.

"Chief Moose?" said Possum.

"Yes, Chief Moose," said Chief Moose.

"Come in, Chief Moose," said Possum. "I'm just putting on the kettle for a cup of tea."

Chief Moose stepped inside. "Just what I need," he said.
"I was passing by and thought to myself, 'I bet Possum is
putting on the kettle for a cup of tea.' So I knocked on
your door, and what do you know…"

"I was just putting on the kettle for—"

"Exactly," said Chief Moose.

"You look tired, Chief Moose," said Possum.

"Tired I am, Possum. So many come to me with their problems and their questions. Seems like some days there's no let-up."

"I don't know what we all would do without you, Chief," said Possum. "Sit here in my best and most comfortable chair, and put your hooves up. Would you care for a hot buttered scone to go with your cup of tea?"

"With marmalade or strawberry jam?"

"Of course. Which would you prefer?"

Chief Moose had no sooner taken his first bite of scone and marmalade and his first sip of tea than there came another knock on Possum's door.

"Who is it?" said Possum.

"It's me, Wolverine," said Wolverine.

"Wolverine?" said Possum.

"Yes, Wolverine," said Wolverine.

Possum opened the door. "I hear that Chief Moose is here," said Wolverine, pushing his way in. "I have a question for him."

Possum said, "Sit down, Wolverine, and I will bring you a cup of tea."

Wolverine sat beside Chief Moose.

"What is your question, Wolverine?" asked Chief Moose.

"Chief Moose, you know The Great Forest better than anyone," said Wolverine, "so I have a question for you.

I am thinking of leaving Nannycatch and going to live in Pussytoe Hollow. My question is: What are the creatures like, the ones who live in Pussytoe Hollow? Are they friendly and helpful and easy to get along with, like me?"

Possum handed Wolverine a cup of tea and a scone. Wolverine looked over at Chief Moose's plate. "Doesn't marmalade come with this?" he asked Possum rudely.

"Of course," said Possum, "or strawberry jam. Take your pick."

"Supersize me on the jam," said Wolverine, "and bring another scone while you're at it."

The Chief pursed his lips. "Let me ask you a question, Wolverine. How do you like everyone here in Nannycatch? Are they friendly and helpful and easy to get along with?"

"I don't like them at all, Chief. They are not easy to get along with. They are the reason I wish to leave."

Possum placed a second plate, with the extra scone and jam, in front of Wolverine.

Chief Moose said, "The answer to your question, Wolverine, is that Pussytoe Hollow is no better than Nannycatch. In fact, there is very little difference. I don't think you will like it one little bit."

"Thank you, Chief. If Pussytoe Hollow is not suitable, then I must try to think of someplace else."

Wolverine abruptly finished his tea and scone and left.

"Have another cup of tea, Chief," said Possum.

"Thank you, Possum. You are most kind."

No sooner had Chief Moose taken a sip of his second cup of tea than there came another knock at the door.

"Who is it?" said Possum.

"It's me, Porcupine," said Porcupine.

"Porcupine?" said Possum.

"Yes, Porcupine," said Porcupine.

Possum opened the door.

"Good morning, Possum," said Porcupine. "Isn't it a beautiful day? Wolverine tells me that Chief Moose is here. Do you think I might come in for a minute or two?"

"Of course," said Possum. "Sit down, and I will bring you a cup of tea."

"That is most kind of you, indeed, Possum. I will take it black with one lump of sugar if you don't mind and if it's no trouble."

"No trouble at all," said Possum.

Porcupine sat beside Chief Moose. "I am trying to decide whether to leave Nannycatch and go live in Pussytoe Hollow to be closer to my brother. My question is: What are they like, the folk who live in Pussytoe Hollow? Are they courteous, helpful and kind?"

Possum handed Porcupine a cup of tea.

"Thank you, Possum. Most kind of you."

"Not at all," said Possum. "Would you like a scone with a little jam or home-made marmalade?"

"Baked in your own oven, I'm sure," said Porcupine, his eyes twinkling. "How can I refuse? With marmalade, please."

The Chief said, "Let me ask you a question, Porcupine. Do you find everyone here in Nannycatch courteous, helpful and kind?"

"Yes, indeed, Chief Moose. They are the finest creatures in the whole of The Great Forest."

"Then the answer to your question, Porcupine, is that you will like Pussytoe Hollow also. It is much like Nannycatch Meadows. In fact there is little difference between them. I am certain that you will like it there."

"Thank you, Chief. That decides it: I will move to Pussytoe Hollow first thing tomorrow morning. My brother and his family will be delighted." He turned to Possum. "Thank you so much for the tea. Everything was delicious."

When Porcupine had gone, Chief Moose said to Possum, "Thanks for the tea, Possum. Porcupine is right: your scones are truly delicious."

"You're entirely welcome, Chief," said Possum. "Please drop by any time."

CHAPTER 12

LiFE

Badger was missing.

He had gone foraging for food for his family yesterday evening—beechnuts and succulent horsetail roots and honey from the hive and whatever else he could find— and had failed to return.

"He never stays away for more than a few hours at a time," said Badger's wife, frantic with worry. "What will I do if he does not return? And my five tiny babies— what will become of them?"

It was not long before the grass told the birds, who told the trees, who told Wind, and soon everyone in The Great Forest knew that Badger was caught in a leghold trap in a place called Bootle Mallett, not too far from Boggle Hole.

The sun had been up only a short time, and the day was still cool. Chief Moose took a rescue squad with him,

Possum and his friends, who brought food and water. He also took along Marten of Biskey Fen, who carried two stout oak staffs to pry open the jaws of the trap. Marten knew a lot about traps; he had lost two uncles, a nephew and a sister-in-law to legholds.

When the rescue party got to Bootle Mallett, they found Badger caught fast in the sharp, vicious teeth of the trap. He was barely alive. Both hind legs were broken and torn and he had lost a lot of blood. He was almost too weak to drink.

The sight of Badger's suffering made Robin weep.

Marten and Chief Moose struggled with the trap, working the oak staffs to release him. It took a long time, but finally Badger was free. Possum and Chipmunk helped lift Badger up onto Chief Moose's back, and they took him home to his den.

Badger's wife burst into tears when she saw the father of her children bloody and broken.

Chief Moose carried Badger inside and laid him on his bed. "Bind his broken limbs with stout branches," he ordered. "But be careful; already his wounds are swollen with infection."

"Make sure he drinks plenty of tea," Chipmunk advised.

"Bathe his head to bring down his fever," said Raccoon.

Possum knew that drinking tea and head bathing would not be enough to save poor Badger, especially if his wounds were infected. Something more powerful was needed, but what? He went outside to think. He paced up and down. He thought of his Grandfather Possum, now deceased, a great apothecary who had discovered the healing powers of ordinary herbs and plants. Possum looked up at the sky. "Help me, Grandfather," he begged. "Badger is my friend. I cannot see him die. Help me make him well."

He waited. The sky was silent.

Then he felt something, a tingling in his blood. He knew at once that it was the spirit of his grandfather flowing through him. He closed his eyes until the tingling had stopped, and then he marched back into Badger's den. Everyone gathered around Badger's bed.

"Stand back and give him some air," said Possum gently. He examined Badger. The torn and broken areas of Badger's hind legs were badly infected, sure enough. The longer Possum waited, the worse the infection would become.

"I will make medicine to cure the infection." He looked around at his friends. "But I will need some help." He sent his friends to gather plants and herbs while he prepared a sterile area near the bed. Soon his helpers were bringing a variety of fresh green stems, grasses and leaves from The Great Forest.

Possum set to work pressing together flowers and leaves of blood-wort, St. John's wort and stickwort, and poured

their juices into a pan set over a low heat. Then, with a mortar and pestle, he pounded and pulped chanterelle and shaggy-mane mushrooms, milkweed and mugwort, prickly poppy and yarrow, maidenhair fern and deer's tongue, monkshood and baneberry. He scraped the mixture into the pan and added stems of ragweed and marsh mallow. He turned up the heat a little and added slivers of dandelion and burdock. When the mixture began to bubble, he added chopped leaves of pussytoes and dogbane.

Badger's den filled with a strange and wonderful aroma.

Possum's friends watched, whispering excitedly among themselves. They had never seen anything quite like this before.

"It's ready," said Possum finally.

Noses twitched and sniffed.

"Delightful," said Squirrel.

"Delicious," said Chipmunk.

Possum poured the medicine from the pan into a bottle and held it up to the light. The liquid was clear and golden. He held the bottle to Badger's mouth. Badger gulped the medicine down.

"Now it's time for him to rest," said Possum, wiping his brow, "while the medicine does its work."

Everyone moved outside to lie in the tall grass and watch the sun climb slowly into the sky. Possum was just nodding off to sleep when Badger's wife came running out of her den. She was smiling. "The swellings and the fever have gone," she cried.

The medicine had worked. Possum whispered his thanks to the sky.

Everyone tiptoed in. Chief Moose examined the patient. He smiled. "Badger is going to be all right."

"BADGER IS SAVED!" said Pigeon.

Robin wiped away a tear of joy.

Chief Moose thanked Possum, Marten and everyone else for working so hard to save Badger's life. Then Squirrel and Chipmunk made several pots of tea and two heaped plates of parsley and watercress sand- wiches for every- one, which they had outside on the grass.

By now the sun was high: it was the afternoon.

Dormouse sighed and said, "Life in The Great Forest is good."

Beaver, unaccustomed to sitting around idly, was fidgety. "I should be getting back to work," he mur- mured to himself.

Uncle Possum, who had arrived late, ate too many parsley and watercress sandwiches and fell asleep, snoring loudly.

Chief Moose said, "Badger's mother-in-law is coming tomorrow from Pokey Edge to help nurse Badger."

Raccoon looked up at the sky and said, "Badger will be walking again by the time the leaves are ready to fall from the trees; I am sure of it."

"Yes, indeed," said Robin. "Badger has a strong fighting spirit."

"And a fine sense of humour," said Raccoon. "He will soon be making up his funny riddles again."

"Yes," said Otter, "like the one about Mole and Moose."

"I don't know that one," said Chipmunk.

Otter said, "What do you get if you cross Mole with Moose?"

"Search me," said Chipmunk.

"Very large holes all through The Great Forest," said Otter.

Everyone laughed politely and drank more tea. The afternoon wore on. Squirrel and Chipmunk made more parsley and watercress sandwiches.

"I wish to propose a toast to Badger's courage," said Possum, as the sun began its descent over the treetops. He held his teacup aloft.

"Badger's courage!" chorused his friends, lifting their cups.

Otter waved his cup. "And a toast to Possum, the best medicine maker in all of The Great Forest."

"To Possum!" everyone shouted.

Uncle Possum heard the name "Possum," woke up, saw the raised teacups and thought they were toasting him. "Thank you, thank you," he said and went immediately back to sleep.

Possum and Chipmunk refilled everyone's teacups. "One last toast, my friends," said Possum. He held up his teacup. "To Life."

"To Life!" said the others in unison.

Soon it was time for everyone to go. Badger was sleeping soundly. They said goodbye to Badger's family.

Possum walked home with Chipmunk. It had been a long day; they were tired; neither one of them had much to say, except "Goodnight" as they parted at the little wooden bridge over the beck.

Possum made himself a cup of tea, took it up to his roof and looked out over Nannycatch Meadows and the sea beyond. He sighed contentedly. *Dormouse is right*, he thought. *Life is good. Life is a gift.* He sipped his tea. Sun dipped her toes in the sea, tossing golden streamers over The Great Forest. Swallows swooped low over Possum's roof. Late-working honey-bees fumbled the flowers; tired butterflies fluttered in the grass. Fragrant breezes stirred the leaves of the old oak tree. The blessings of The Great Forest lay all about.

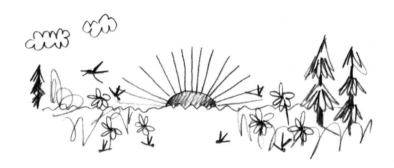